Look What I Found!

by Michaela Muntean
Illustrated by John Costanza

Featuring Jim Henson's
Sesame Street Muppets

A SESAME STREET/GOLDEN PRESS BOOK
Published by Western Publishing Company, Inc.
in conjunction with Children's Television Workshop.

Early one morning, Ernie and Bert and Big Bird and Betty Lou and Grover and the Count climbed aboard a big orange bus. They were going to the national forest for a nature walk.

"I brought a bag along to hold the things I find in the forest," said Ernie.

"I brought my sketch book," said Betty Lou, "so I can draw pictures."

"I brought binoculars so I can see birds high up in the trees," said Big Bird.

"I brought peanut butter and banana sandwiches for our picnic," said Grover.

"I brought a notebook so I can write
down all the wonderful things I find to count,"
said the Count.

"I brought this nature book. It will
tell us all about the things we see in the
forest," said Bert.

The bus drove away from Sesame
Street and out of the city. Soon there were no
more big buildings or shops or stores.

Finally, the bus stopped at the entrance to the forest trail.

"Smell that fresh air," said Ernie. "Listen to the birds singing. Look at the red and gold leaves on the trees. Autumn is here and we are here to see it!"

"Let's go!" said Bert. "Let's see what special things we can find in the forest."

NATIONAL FOREST

Ernie was the first
to find something. "Look!"
he called. "I found the
reddest leaf in the whole
world. Isn't it beautiful?"

"Yes, Ernie," said Bert. "It's a maple
leaf that fell from that maple tree."

Ernie dropped the leaf into his bag.

"Look what I found!" Grover cried. "It is fuzzy and soft and cute like me. It is a green baby monster sleeping under this tree."

"No, that is moss," Bert said, opening his book. "Moss is a tiny, leafy plant that grows in damp places," he read.

"I think I'll take some home with me," said Ernie.

"Look!" Betty Lou exclaimed. "Doesn't that look like a walking rock?"

"Yes, but it's not a rock. It's a turtle," said Bert. "A turtle carries his shell with him all the time," he read. "When he wants to hide from an enemy or go to sleep, he pulls his head, feet, and tail into his shell. A turtle's shell is his home."

"I see another home," Big Bird said. "It's a nest just like mine, but much, much smaller."

"One wonderful nest!" cried the Count. He wrote 'one nest' in his notebook.

"Look," said Betty Lou. "Maybe the nest belongs to that bird."

"That's a robin," said Bert, looking in his book. "It is gray with a red breast." Everyone took a turn looking through the binoculars.

"Wow!" said Big Bird. "Look over there—
a giant pincushion!"

"That's a porcupine," Bert explained.
"The 'pins' are really quills to protect him
from bigger animals."

Ernie started to pick a leaf
from a plant.

"Stop, Ernie!" cried Bert.
"That's poison ivy. Don't touch it
or it will make your skin red and
itchy. Here's a picture of it in my
book. 'Leaves of three, let it be.'"

"What about leaves of four?" the Count asked. "This little plant has one...two... three...four little leaves."

"That's a four-leaf clover," Betty Lou said. "Four-leaf clovers are hard to find. Some people think they bring good luck."

The Count gave the clover to Ernie to put in his bag.

"Look what I found!" Betty Lou cried. "Dandelion puffs."

"What's this nut, Bert?" asked Big Bird.

"That's an acorn," Bert answered. "Acorns are the seeds of oak trees."

"It looks too little to grow into something so big," Big Bird said.

"Look! Ten wonderful footprints!"
cried the Count.

"Those are rabbit tracks," Bert said.

"And there goes the rabbit, right into those
bushes. Let's follow his tracks and see where
he's going," said Betty Lou.

They went through the
bushes and came out into a clearing
by a stream.

"The bunny found a beautiful
place for our picnic," said Grover.

They spread a cloth on the
grass and Grover got out the
sandwiches he had brought.

"Look at the berries I found!" Betty Lou said. "Can we have them for dessert, Bert?"

"We must be careful about eating things we find in the forest," said Bert. "Some berries are poisonous and will make you sick." He looked in his book. "Those are wild strawberries," he said. "They are safe to eat."

A beautiful butterfly landed on Big Bird's beak.

"That's a monarch butterfly," Bert read from his book.

"Hold still, Big Bird," said Betty Lou. "I want to draw a picture of the butterfly."

Suddenly they heard something behind them. They turned around and saw two furry animals splashing in the stream.

"Raccoons!" Bert said. "They are washing their food before they eat it."

Finally it was time to go home. They all started walking back the way they had come.

"I found some terrific things for my nature collection today," said Ernie. "I have a maple leaf and some moss and a porcupine quill and a four-leaf clover and an acorn."

"And here is a pine cone for you, Ernie," said Big Bird.

"I drew pictures
of a turtle, a porcupine,
a rabbit, and a butterfly,"
said Betty Lou.

"We saw raccoons
and strawberries and
dandelion puffs," said
the Count.

"And a nest and a
robin," said Big Bird.

"And poison ivy,"
said Bert.

"Goodbye, forest!" called
Big Bird as they rode away in
the bus. "Thank you for such a
nice day. We'll come again soon."

ABCDEFGHI